Souvenirs

SOUVENIRS

Andrew E. Colarusso

Karen An-hwei Lee

BAOBAB PRESS

Table of Contents

Watch I

I left Nautilus Island with a watch purported to have belonged to the great poet, long dead but alive in the worn wood characteristic of that place. Despite a complete lack of authentifying documentation, the guy who sold it to me insisted it belonged to the poet because "Looksee here on the band, it's inscribed with his initials if you don't believe me. Fact is I knew his mother. She and I sat for supper every Wednesday in her latter years and I guess she trusted me enough to bequeath this watch. I said I'd never sell it but here we are. Hard times on the Island. Hauling nothing but trash these days. These nets crying for something other than plastic."

Whether any of this was true barely mattered after the fact of the transaction.

Two things had become abundantly clear to me in the days before leaving. 1: Hard times had indeed fallen on Nautilus Island. It had become a shell of its former economic glory and its once noble culture survived in matte-finish postcards and tall tales told over imported chowder. And this 2: is exactly what I loved about Nautilus Island. It was a ghost town—one that, at least for me, meant the celebration of an old, imperious guard doomed by its own unselfconscious hubris. The Island, as far as I was concerned, had become a monument to the inner-workings of something like the moral arc of the universe. Nautilus Island was dying, or had died already. Long may it live.

Realizing these two things, I felt, before leaving, a sudden urge to collect parts of a place that confirmed the righteous violence of my (our) own existence—just one memento mori from a place that seemed oddly prepossessing for someone in search of home. Wandering the cobblestone alleys of Old Town (what they called the historic district) on my last gray day, I found the curio shop.

"My father," continued the fisherman-proprietor, "was a Bishop at the Presbyterian church here. Never took to those rollicking Baptists. But he was a good man and he knew well the poet's mother. I spent most of my time then at sea. And the poet, close to my age, a little younger, went pussy-footing all over, selling the pastoral dream of our little piece of earth to anyone who would listen. Beautiful poems, sure. But he had no idea what it was really like to live here. And he certainly wasn't here for the Great Perishing." The old man ran his bony fingers through a fox stain shock of hair. "So I have no particular attachment to this old thing—despite a general affection for his late mother. May she rest in peace. You ask me, old man McNabb—*he* was a poet. Get some nectar in him and he'd rattle off the most profane, life transforming lyrics this side of wherever." He laughed and I smiled and pulled out my wallet. "I'm the last of my kin," he said, processing the payment. "What would I need this watch for?"

I think I know what he meant.

Waiting on the portal-out, I found an empty bench at the end of the platform and let myself, for those last moments on Nautilus Island, admire the entirety of my experience in the face of that watch. It was handsome. Old, yes, but sturdy and functional. More than anything, it seemed the perfect souvenir—a strangely sentient witness of my having been here, having fallen in love with the memory of a mark against my humanity—and what could or would happen to any such living denial. So enamored with my find, I hadn't noticed the anxious-looking man in skins and trench-slip when he sat beside me on the bench.

"You got the time?" he asked, eyeing the watch.

"I'm sorry," I replied, "my watch doesn't tell time."

The stranger looked unamused. "What does your watch tell, then?"

"It measures distance." I explained. "Vectors."

He must've thought I was kidding because he shot right up and walked away shaking his head. I suppose he couldn't imagine a watch that measured the distance between vectors—the magnitude and direction of objects in relation to the wearer of the watch. The stranger who sat beside me: six minutes and quickly redshifting away from me. The old man who sold me the watch: eight hours back and blue. And you: you were three years, two months, two weeks, three days and getting redder by the second.

Photographer's Cloth

Fluttering like an origami moth in the city of moonlit facades, the photographer's cloth takes flight over the heads of children on their way home from evening rehearsals at the conservatory: the string quartets, the classical woodwinds like flutes and clarinets and oboes, the chamber orchestras with little fleets of violins, violas, and cellists, and of course, the lone bass trombone. A clandestine photographer ducks under his cloth; it looks as if a shapeshifting shadow sidles along the wall, an object of polymorphism: origami dove, a lotus, a frog, and a paper grasshopper of sixteen folds.

Rush hour stands still for a minute as the photographer's cloth drags its ragged shadow across the sidewalks, through the streetlights. The algorithms of the city's information engines and heat-seeking drones scour the grids for used clothes, textiles and fabrics for shoots, responses to questions about why photographers wear black, what to wear in a darkroom, pants for photographers, and clothing for wildlife photography in the city like bats and pigeons.

So the tale goes, a soul—which cannot be photographed, for it has no surfaces other than the flesh which anchors its being to this world—projects a curious shadow in this millennium. Call it a vestige of turn-of-century imperial ghosts; call it the alienation of humans from the means of production; blame it on data insects called bots; call it the mechanization of thought in the fourth industrial revolution; or call it the shot-off wings of a man-moth whose visage is rarely seen in daylight, one whose tears emerge from a wellspring under the city.

Once, I saw the soul riding a bicycle in the air as if in a dream.

It was a vapor released out of an invisible perfume jar, a transparent vase without an actual vessel, yet imparting fragrant traces of ethers and esters: the scent of a breath. Or let's call it a dream of levitation in an era where jet propulsion—backwards, at that—is the prevailing *modus operandi* of the age.

Let me start this tale again, if I may.

Once upon a time, a photographer's cloth trailed from the shoulders of the man whose frail body anchored his soul to this realm of life. Draped and folded like a dress made of crepe roses with a long train, soiled by the silt of subway rails and artificial tunnels, it nodded quietly in the flickering nocturnal wind, honoring the memory of faded souvenirs like the old-fashioned daguerreotype and camera obscura.

Does the cloth recall the aroma of wild strawberries ripening in the mountains? Does it feel nostalgic about summers by the creek of darting minnows in the afternoon light? What does it cherish about this earthbound journey, and the eventual passage to an afterlife? It hears the rustling of grass soon to wither, already passing to fade—or else singed in a raging brushfire— and photographs the color of sepia and champagne, which tell no story at all unless we remember the lives of those who sat for the photographer.

String

Three-tiered Mistral Monastery at the peak of Mont Daumal was widely rumored for the sui generis variety of string instrument produced there. Monks and Nuns of the order were said to have co-existed in the rare, thin air of that place, each trained in some aspect of the craft. The most esteemed of these proud and solemn believers handled, exclusively, the strings.

Just so happens, once upon a time, I made it to the top of Mont Daumal and the Monastic Order, as was their custom, let me crash. After administering much needed oxygen, Sister Alice explained to me that I would be allowed a week proper to see for myself what their lives were like and then decide whether I was truly willing to "make such a sacrifice for the renewal of your soul. If you so choose," she continued, "you'll spend at least forty days and nights on the first level of our monastery living among the ascetics—those who've renounced all worldly ways in favor of the supersymmetric. Do you understand?" Still lightheaded and unable to speak through the oxygen mask, I nodded once in the affirmative.

So began my week of consideration. Sister Alice showed me to a spartan visitor's chamber and pointed out the oxygen tank by the nightstand, in case of sudden lightheadedness or palpitations. "The Monastery," she reminded before leaving, "is open for exploration. You'll find no door locked. Tomorrow morning, Father Sogol shall take you for a proper tour. In the meantime, I suggest you rest. Meals will be served promptly at the second bell. Restroom and shower down the hall." And she was right. I was more exhausted than my adrenaline-induced ascent led me to believe. After two weeks of carefully considered climbing and camping, I'd reached the summit of a peradam purported not to have existed at all—and now all I wanted was rest. I sank into an armchair by the window and stared out at a sea of clouds before falling asleep.

////\ • /\\\\

Father Sogol arrived at first light to find me at the foot of the bed wheezing into an oxygen mask. He laid a hand on my shoulder and, in a voice softer than his wrinkles suggested, said, "Breathe slowly, my son. Your heart will learn to do more with less." Then he knelt, maybe to inspect the crisis in my face, and he smiled an oddly comforting black-toothed smile. Slowly he slid the mask from my face until it was off entirely and with a hand on my back he reminded, "Breathe slowly and from the belly. You'll be fine." He withdrew what looked like a bluish banana from a pocket of his brown robe and instructed me to eat while we walked. This particular "fruit" (that tasted like a full Thanksgiving dinner), he mentioned, was chock full of beta blockers and tryptophan. Barring my quiet shock at both the unusual taste of this fruit and Father Sogol's liberal language, I followed the old man to our first destination, the Court of Owls.

The only way I can think to describe the architecture: an inverted pagoda carved three stories deep into the peak of the mountain. At the center of the first and widest of these tiers, where lived newcomers and ascetics, was a still, silvery pool surrounded by birch trees. "This," said Father Sogol, "is the Court of Owls." Perched in the topmost branches of the trees, their leaves aflame without burning, were ghostly owls. These owls were ever so slightly transparent and their heads seemed to spin frantically in all directions. Before I could ask Father Sogol what it was I had seen, he jumped into the silvery pool at the heart of the court and disappeared. "Father Sogol?" I asked, half-aware that I'd spoken so softly and with such trepidation no one could hear. I crept toward the mercurial pool and peered over its shiny edge when, all at once, the ghostly owls ceased their head-spinning and fixed their spectral eyes on me. I took that as my cue to follow. I jumped in.

////\ • /\\\\

I landed in what looked like a cellar. Father Sogol stood before a waist-high wooden cabinet and motioned me near. "Of course you're here because you've heard of our psalteries. Yes?"

"Yes," I replied. "I've heard fascinating stories about the instruments you make here. But I've never seen one."

"This is where we keep the string for our psalteries."

In each of the two cabinet doors were installed windows with criss-crossing muntins between which I could see shimmering three silvered strings.

"Unlike other psaltery instruments, our strings are not made of metal, but a kind of gut found in cats particular to this part of the world. These three are to be used in the production of our next psaltery. All of us here have access to the materials necessary to craft the instrument. The wood for the soundboard. The varnish. The string. But few among us are actually qualified to handle the string."

The cabinet, to my surprise, was held shut with nothing more than a bit of red thread. No lock. And I'm not sure if I was imagining this, but I could feel the cabinet . . . humming?

"Why," I asked, "are only a few qualified to handle the string?"

"Because it's really mysterious. That's why. What kind of dumb question?"

"Forgive me, Father, but what kind of music does this instrument make anyway?"

"The alchemic music of the cosmos. I thought you already knew about this."

"I mean, I only heard stories. I didn't know any details . . ."

"Good. Let's move on to the Garden of Perpetual Twilight."

So I followed him to the Garden of Perpetual Twilight, but couldn't help wondering what he meant by *alchemic music of the cosmos.*

////\ • /\\\\

That night I decided I'd return to the cabinet, just to see the string. I crept out into the Court of Owls, their heads still spinning, and dove into the silvery pool that would take me to the string room. I sat with my legs crossed before the cabinet as it hummed through the wood and into my body, until the hum enveloped me and I felt suddenly possessed to open the cabinet. I unknotted the red thread that held the cabinet shut and edged closer to the glowing middle string which seemed, like the ghostly owls, to have been there and *not* there. The strings on either side seemed to hum sympathetically and together the three danced oddly in their casing as though living things. Lord forgive me, all I wanted to do was touch them, feel for what made them hum so impossibly. And I figured, I've come all this way; would be a shame not to know. So I gently plucked the middle string and it seemed to vibrate at frequencies in and out and all around as urgent and pleasing as the unplanned nearness of the one whose heart you desire and whose breath you suddenly and for the first time taste at the river's edge before sharing the kiss that marks the start of your lives together. And when it stopped vibrating I found myself here with nothing more than the clothes on my back and the plain, red thread that held the cabinet shut.

So, yeah. It definitely exists. This here's proof positive.

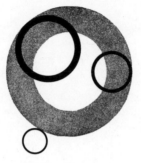

Flock

The flock dreams of this and such about a feast yet to come.

The flock dreams of the end of the world without fear. The collective term for sheep is either flock or mob—striking contrasts in apparent usage—although synonymous in this context. Every member of the flock, blanketed in a little bit of love yet sore with hunger and the aching world of yore, sees angels of the future aflame with their flashing swords, gesturing to the golden path to eternity. In response, the flock slowly backs up over a hill into the meadow.

They're not afraid of eternity; rather, it's a fear of the uncertain.

Will it hurt, psychologically, to pass through life to the other side? What process will involve shedding their bodies, or what policies will govern the acquisition of new flesh through bodily transformation? A seamless metamorphosis or quick sloughing? Their wool, shorn of thistles and burrs, sends a light frisson over their shin bones, grazing the unspun tenderness of lilies.

A shadow of the pastoral drives the flock to the meadow,

then the field of a setting sun. The flock bleats with the pleasure of wild lilies, with radical contentment. Is the flock aware of its own existence flowing in a parcel of stardust, the grit of the universe—digested in the belly of a ruminant creature like a sheep? The flock, or at least a small part of it, bleats as it falls into creeks and ditches, and the shepherds run to fish them out like bales of cotton with legs. In the distance, a lightning storm passes over the hills, so the flock gathers under a tree.

The flock doesn't know whether it should huddle under a cottonwood, white pine, a stand of poplars, or sycamore. It doesn't understand electrostatic charge. The flock also doesn't see the differences between the risk of danger and the impulse of beauty, and cannot gauge how lightning might strike the tree at any moment. The storm passes without harm, thanks to God who responds to the prayers of the shepherds, ever vigilant among the boulders.

In a dream of the flock, the sheep—streaked and brindled with hazel—wait for God to make an entrance on the stage of the world. A meadow, a hill, a pasture. God will show up in the form of a sheep, they know this shivering in their inner bones, and not only a sheep but a little lamb. The sheep believe he'll show up in the end times, bleating right out of his mother's womb, ready to share some astonishing news. He's the one, and no one else, says the lamb.

Do I have clods of wax in my ears?

How can this be? Do you believe? In a matter of seasons, the lamb is sacrificed for chops although he hasn't done anything egregiously wrong, and shortly thereafter, ascends to heaven. Women are the first ones to witness the evidence of resurrection. Was this due to their willingness to pay attention to possibilities in life, or their willingness to wait and see? An angel speaks to the women in translation: By the way, if you haven't heard already, there's salvation for souls through this lamb who remains mute before his shearers, who glows like a night light equipped with cloven hooves, and ultimately, shines with ruminant radiance, chewing the cud before his reckless butchers.

The rest of the sheep will be scattered for a time until the shepherds see the lamb appear to them for a little while, standing on a beach. They'll calm down for a minute, then go to the ends of the earth, generation after generation. Indeed, the flocks and their descendants of ensuing generations will fry lamb chops in remembrance of him, then squabble about whether the chops are his figurative or actual elements, in other words, the phenomenon of consubstantiation or transubstantiation.

No mint jelly is provided for these chops, mind you. This is serious business, not a gourmand's review of an upscale bistro. Don't believe anyone who tells you that mint jelly is essential, or worse, tries to sell jars of mint condiment for a mint. Moreover, the lamb chops are rather pricey, not to mention forbidden to vegetarians, so the flocks decide to use wafers instead, which can also be made of rice flour, gluten-free.

Just trying to kill two birds with one stone, the generations say.

God says to the generations, your theology and your doctrine, your dickering back and forth in your debates, strayed far from the words I gave you through my beloved lamb.

The generations reply, there's more of us than you, and besides, we have to deal with one another on a daily basis, moment by moment. Why should we pay attention to your command to love you and one another when such travesties of war and bloodshed and plague and global warming go unabated on the face of this earth you created?

God says, who said I created those things?

The generations reply, you allow them.

God says, you gave me leave, so I gave you room.

The generations reply, there's no more room.

God says, this is the earth you made, not mine.

The generations reply, show yourself to us.

God says, this little lamb is the one.

Now the sound of the evening bells calls the flock home in a simple hymn, and shepherds listen to the murmur of the sheep as they wind their way across the meadows.

Gazeless

"I'm an actor," he said. "Sort of."

"Sort of?"

"Voice actor. It's what pays the bills. You know."

"Ah," I said, trying to mask my disappointment. Another actor. "I won't hold it against you."

But this time, I couldn't help wanting to hold it against him. He seemed to have all the charm and charisma of a green-screen star, but none of the psychosis. His voice was full and his gaze direct in a way that felt non-confrontational. He was without that desperate reek most men seemed to secrete when bested by their desire to have it all. Honestly, I couldn't pick up on a mask or some skeevy scheme. He was just kind of lovely. And maybe that was true cause for concern.

"What's it like? Being a voice actor."

"It's cool. It's fun work. I don't have to be center stage. I walk into an air-conditioned studio and spit out a few lines in my heavenly voice and they send me a check. The taxes of which I'll end up paying for later, but whatever. It's good work."

"So what you're saying is, you're 100 percent aware that your voice is as appealing as it is."

"It's the one compliment I get from strangers."

I found that hard to believe. He was as handsome as his voice was heavenly. Objectively speaking, he seemed like the kind of man any woman would at least consider dating material. He was tall. At first glance you could've mistaken him for frail, but he was just a lanky guy. Even sitting. With salt and pepper hair. Autumnal eyes, one pupil oddly wider than the other, and crow's feet that made it look like he was smiling all the time.

"Sorry. All of that probably sounded really arrogant. What I mean to say is, I've managed to make a living off this kind of stuff, but I don't consider it a vocation."

What he meant as a humbled clarification almost sounded more pretentious. But something about him nevertheless felt sincere. Or was it that I *wanted* to trust him? "So what is your vocation?"

"It's embarrassing. I guess I'm just another failed artist in a town full of failed or failing artists. I'm an amateur photographer. And a writer. I like to tell people's stories. I like close portraits and close reads on the minutest complexities of life."

"Why is that embarrassing?"

"Because no one gives a rip about my stuff. It's like Anne Carson has this killer moment in one of her pieces. *My personal poetry is a failure. / I do not want to be a person. / I want to be unbearable.*"

We had a table by the window. The trees were turning. No longer late summer, but verging on winter. Those beautiful oak reds and gingko golds had become brittle, the branches beginning to show bare. There had already been a morning frost. And my skin this time of year, cold and dry and cracked, carried a perpetual charge that left me vulnerable to alarming jolts of static shock from anything vaguely electric. Light switches especially inspired dread. This was, for me, a sure sign of the season's approach.

"Anyway," he said, noticing my attention elsewhere, "what about you? Tell me about yourself."

"I like long walks and holidays at the Cape."

"Funny lady."

He took my cheek in stride. Then continued prodding.

"Do you have family?"

"I do."

"Kids?"

"A sister."

"Older? Younger?"

"Younger."

"Are you—"

"Close? Yes. She's my person in this world."

"What's she like?"

"She's an enigma. Strange. Melancholy. Ambitious, but sometimes blighted by her own defeatism. Talented like none I've ever encountered. Sensitive. But loyal. My God is she loyal. And funny."

"Do you feel comfortable sharing a story about her?"

"Not really. No. You wouldn't understand the idiosyncratic kind of humor we share. A lot of irony. When we're together, things get super po-mo. But when I stop and think about how kind she is, how funny and weird. I could almost cry. She's a gem. I will say this, though, just to give you a sense of who she is. After she stopped dancing, she picked up pottery. Kintsugi. And she made the most beautiful, black jade jars from shards of the stuff. She's an artist in that way. She restores and beautifies broken things. Broken people."

"You should text her," he said with such spontaneous enthusiasm I considered acting on his overfamiliar suggestion. "Life's too short not to say the things we mean to say. Right?"

"Yea alright. I haven't texted her today. Might as well drop a line." I pulled out my phone and shot off a quick note. She liked to take her time getting back, so I knew not to hold my breath.

"What did you text her?" he asked.

"I said 'hey babe proud of you xoxo.' Nothing too fancy."

"That's sweet. What does she do?"

"I'm sorry," I said. "I thought we were on a date. If I knew you were this interested in my sister, I would've stayed home."

"Hah," (he actually said hah). "Sorry. I keep putting my foot in my mouth. I just. She seems very important to you. So I wanted to know about her and you and your relationship. All that good stuff."

"She's a dancer. Or she was a dancer."

"What happened?"

"I would rather not talk about it."

After that we sat for a while in silence. Me gazing out the window. Him blowing volutes of steam from his mug. It wasn't uncomfortable silence. Just kind of meditative. A moment for the silt to settle and the waters to clear before starting again. And when it had settled, he was first to break the silence.

"Hey, this might be a bit weird," he started, reaching into his pocket, "but, do you recognize this?"

He slid what looked like a used Band-Aid across the table, a yellowed spot on the gauze where blood had separated. Fortunately I didn't have to state the obvious before he apologized. Maybe it was the look of disgust or incredulity. I've had worse dates, but never a used bandage at a café.

"Sorry again," he said, "this must be very weird and obviously unhygienic. But let me explain?" He flipped the bandage, gauze side down, revealing a colorful cartoon print on the band. "You recognize it now."

He wasn't asking. He knew I recognized it. My favorite cartoon. Our favorite cartoon. She used these to bandage her toes when she was still doing pointe. Then she used them to cover the incision scars after the diagnosis.

"Where did you get this?" I asked. "Is this some kind of sick joke? Did you do something to my sister, you maniac? I will end your life right now. Don't test me."

"Your sister is fine."

"Then how did you get this? Some kind of stalker? Blackmail? What's your angle here? Speak up now or this is about to get ugly."

"It's not your sister," he said. "It's *you.*"

A surprise.

I spoke into his eyes, "I thought?"

"You died alone a long time ago."

"I'm calling the cops."

I pulled out my phone, got up from the table, and felt the hot rush of anger replaced suddenly by a cold wave of unease and fear when I realized our café was empty. My phone, suddenly without reception.

"Think about it," he said. "Do you remember having come here? To this café?"

No, I couldn't remember.

"Please sit. Let me explain."

"No way. You're not gonna gaslight me. I'm getting out of here. And don't bother following."

"Listen, I will leave you alone if you can at least tell me where we are. Better yet. Fine. Just leave. Go ahead. The door's right there."

I ran for the exit, grabbed the handle, pushed it open, dove outside, and found myself sitting right back at the coffee table by the window, voice actor across from me, hands in his lap, a gazeless stare.

"What is this?" I said, about ready to cry.

"That's the thing about falling," he replied. "On this planet, the greater your leap, the more time you have to accelerate toward a force that strikes back in equal and opposite measure. But we don't bounce. In fact, we keep on falling even after all the falling is done. The organs. The heart. The guts. The brain. The eyes. The lungs. They're still falling, until they're suddenly told to go back. Back in the direction they've come from. And that sudden counter-instruction is too much for our fragile human bodies to handle."

"Is that how I died?"

"No. Not quite."

"Who are you?" I asked. But he wouldn't answer.

"Why are we here?"

"There was something I needed you to do," he said.

"What's that?"

"I needed you to text your sister."

"I don't understand. Why?"

He pointed to a television above the bar. How long it'd been there, I had no idea. It was set to Sunday evening news. On screen flashed an old photo, my favorite, of me and my sister as kids. Then came what sounded like my sister's voice. *When they'd diagnosed me and started me on treatment they said there was a 99 percent chance I'd be stuck in a wheelchair the rest of my life. Forget about dance. No chance you come back from this kind of dystrophy. Then I lost my sister. And I thought about taking my life. I bought the stuff. I was committed. But that night I had a dream. In the dream my sister texted me. Just a little note. It said 'hey babe proud of you xoxo' and I knew it was her. I knew it was my sister's spirit telling me to keep going, that I wasn't done. The camera cut to my sister, older than I remembered, but more beautiful. More powerful. Absolutely unafraid. And now here I am. First ever woman with muscular dystrophy to make principal dancer at American Ballet. It's not easy. It's never been easy. Some days I feel so sick, I don't think I can go on. But I have a good group of people behind me, supporting me, encouraging me. More important, I know my sister's proud of me. Yea.*

"Are you dead too?" I asked him.

"Oh, no," he said. "I've never lost control."

"Who are you?" I asked again, face-to-face with a man I couldn't possibly know.

"A friend," he said, sliding the Band-Aid nearer my side of the table.

Incunabula I

You remember, at least, being carried in the dark. Head resting against shoulder. You remember maybe the warmth. And their scent—were it near enough now, the faintest trace of it, how quickly you'd be there again, fallen haplessly into that primordial moment of vulnerability. But you're not thinking of their scent or their warmth per se. It's your sense of the raw, animal muscle that carries you. Torsion of sinew and bone and fat as you feel one arm let go (the other clutching tighter your bottom and back) to reach for and open a door, flip on a light, lay your body down. You remember realizing for the first time what adult strength feels like. Crude and elegant efficiency, the calculus of their careful movement. And now you wonder if that strength is your own. If you are, if you could be, that bulwark in the cold dark that keeps a most vulnerable thing alive.

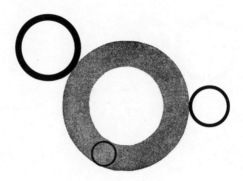

Foil

I drop *foil* into a poem cloud to see what the algorithm generates, like a pebble making ripples in a pond—shook, trod, oil, generations, freshness—if you're wondering, an anagram for *generations* is *tangerine so. Antigens ore. Age intoners. Gentians Roe.* Never words like lily, chocolate, or neuron. I don't mind the garnet noise. Granite nose. Erasing note. Not purely a tinkering game, rather, it's a way of seeing what the rearrangement servant will yield in a cloud. It forges new pathways by visualizing a poem as a form of music wherein the notes are colors, sounds, tones. We're sprung in these rhythms, a smudge of spondees in this organic space opera of biogenesis.

Floating in a miasma of shifting meanings, the recombinant word-sequences dance in a constellation of stars and aromatic black holes. The fragrant nostrils of the universe puff a celestial perfume called poetry. Each time I refresh the cloud at the gentle tap of a button, it regenerates the same words but changes the eye-catching fonts: serif, non-serif, or fonts with the word *freight* in their names. I'm uncertain about dynamic equivalencies when translated into other languages, and whether homonyms and homophones vanish. I don't know whether they refer to other polysemous interactions, or if they're purely denotative.

Did this fragment of foil once cling to the face of a comet? An asteroid? Did its elemental aluminum drop out of the sky, hitting earth after flaring like an amaryllis upon atmospheric entry? I remember the astronauts of yore, encased in their pods, hurtling into the sea. Or is this foil a figurative page of divine glory, torn out of a heavenly tableau?

Curious about the verbal nature of the cloud, I examine the foil to see where it has traveled and where it's headed. I do this to glean what it knows so I may gain from its cosmic journeys. When I ask, how much data is in the universe? The foil replies with trailing ellipsis: *It will flame out . . .* I persist, O foil, what awaits us in the afterlife, when this earthbound journey has ended? *It gathers to a greatness . . .* I pose this question: How do you like dwelling inside this cloud? The foil crinkles with delight, flaming: *The world is charged with the grandeur of God.*

Utterly shook, I kneel.

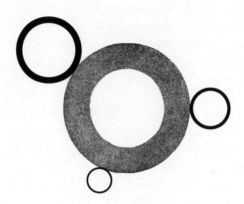

Space Rock

"What happens to books in absolute zero?"

"..."

"You couldn't tell me, could you?"

"..."

"Because how would you know? If I don't know."

"..."

"Paradox."

"..."

"Frankly," said the author, stroking his long white beard, "you know I hate you. I've hated you for a long time now."

"..."

"And I'm tired. Even of the idea that the God of this universe was created by none other than an ordinary man. Limited by his own knowledge." He looked sidelong at his statuesque deity, its glowing white eyes trained on times past, present, and future. "You've nevertheless proven your sentience."

"..."

"Jon," sighed the author, "my poor, fallen idol. You've made a cuckold of me."

Finally fixing his gaze on the author, the idol spoke softly but surely. "You must've known, Alan."

"Known what?"

"What I would become."

"Not really. No. Not until maybe the third issue. I was in any case proud to have written you and the others. And honestly the story was long overdue. The age of hero worship needed its proper funeral. But I hadn't anticipated what would come of it. And I certainly hadn't anticipated the publishers lying to me. The way they did. The way they have. And Dave. And John. Kevin . . ."

"You couldn't have anticipated it. Why do you suppose that is?"

"Because I'm an ordinary man. An ordinary man that gave birth to a god."

"The paradox, if this is to be a paradox, is that I existed well before you put pen to paper, Alan. You are unique, a vessel chosen for your singular capacity to imagine. Extraordinary because only you could've imagined my particular omnipotence incarnate. But you were not alone in the imagining. There was also John, who knew the blueness of my being, and David, who knew my humanoid shape. There have been others since. Zack, Geoff, Gary, Brad, Damon. Others who've tried. But it was you who knew me first. And only you could've known, good and faithful servant—"

"Bravo, Jon!" interrupted the author, shaking his head. "Bravo. Your poetry in the pulpy annals of eighties literature is unparalleled. The fanboys have set their clocks to your return. But please, do tell me what happens to books in absolute zero. Go on. Enlighten us."

The idol, in his blue birthday suit, looked away from the author and stretched out his right hand to reveal a stone, rough and gold in color. "I'm disappointed in you, Alan. I'm very disappointed in you. I have walked across the surface of the sun. I have witnessed events so tiny and fast, they could hardly be said to have happened at all. I have conjured from nothing every possible alloy desired by the alchemists, gold itself forged from my breath, entire planets born at the snap of my fingers. But you, Alan, you're just a writer. The world's smartest comic writer poses no more threat to me than does its smartest squirrel."

The gold nugget hovered and spun an inch or two above his blue palm. Then it stopped spinning and vanished into thin air. The idol too, not a blink later, disappeared, leaving in his wake a small point of blue light that just as quickly faded to nothingness. And the author, for all his familiarity with the otherworldly being he'd first written into existence, couldn't help feeling uneasy when he noticed the sudden jagged weight that'd sunk into his pants pocket. There he found the nugget, a lot lighter than it looked and as cold as an ice cube. For a moment his unease became an unusual titillation—or perhaps, he had to admit, it was excitement. Excitement for the possibility that he had in fact been a vessel for something greater and more infinite than his own imagination. But his excitement quickly gave way to sinking disappointment when he noticed the stone's uniform striations, its hardness.

"Pyrite," he muttered, before tossing the cold stone into a dark corner of his writing desk.

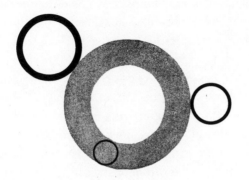

Black Jade

The black jade isn't actually black or jade. It's seaweed or kelp consisting of alginate and soda ash, the ribboned, underwater forests brushing the underside of barges and ferries, caressing the seafaring vessels of tea and clouds alike. You can't use this lump of black jade to carve a large chest of drawers with the semblance of lacquer. You can't use it to fashion the rigging of a yacht or catamaran, but it's as strong. Loosely braided in strands from a rootless thallus, flowing with glassy abandon like a mermaid's unfastened hair, the kelp entangles the legs of swimmers.

Or else the black jade is an image for the mussels in the water. If this tale were a mythopoeia, the seaweed would morph into the severed hair of mermaids who observed the land-dwellers on the beach bluffs, or the sailors on their ships. The seaweed, streaming like hair from mussels, would be compared to black jade. Instead, this box, if you will, is a gift from the sea of time. The ocean swings wide in her hips, a fragrant portal of life.

With the silent motion of undersea angels, of feather stars

and quartz grains of sand, it filters the shafts of light entering. It's not black like the medicinal grass jelly your grandmother served in a porcelain bowl on hot midsummer nights. Neither does it resemble arrowheads and spear points of obsidian glass. It doesn't cool the blood, nor cut to the jugular: black jade has no agenda.

As the hull of my boat glides over the wet forest of black jade, I pull the shadows out of the seawater and knot them around my wrist to protect me as I navigate the channel. *Fish wade through the black jade.* The black jade asks for no sacrifice: rather, it seeks friendship. *Of the crow-blue mussel-shells, one keeps adjusting the ash-heaps; opening and shutting itself like an injured fan.* Who will ensure safety to the creatures journeying through the fathoms of the deep? Presented with this gift, the black jade speaks.

I had a dream where the ancient female bard, recalled from the dead, asked me to translate an ancient poem carved in a lacquered box whose panels depicted mussels, barnacles, crabs, and jellyfish billowing in still life like blossoms from another galaxy. I couldn't read the ciphers, engraved in a lost tongue.

The box says: I am not a box of time.

The black jade replies: A box of the ocean, then.

The box says: I am the box not contained in a poem.

The black jade replies: You are the box in a poem.

The box says: I am not a box.

The black jade replies: I am not a poem, yet I dream.

Stubs

For a driver maneuvering the back roads of an unfamiliar town, a long ride in the dark of night might've felt like being caught in a hail of stray bullets or handing a blank check to a trustworthy creditor. For a navigator intimidated by the smartness of smartphone global positioning, a long ride in the dark of night might've felt like having to disarm a bomb in the nursery (in 10 seconds) while being asked to apologize for every personal misstep (recalculating). For sleepy passengers strapped comfortably in the backseat of a luxury sedan, a long ride in the dark of night might've felt like a gently rocked cradle or the embryonic list and heel of life inside the womb waiting to emerge.

Hard to say what else it might've felt like, but there were 4 of them on their way back to the timeshare after having seen a movie at the local theater. There was the father, who'd gone from *fruit-for-lunch-bunch* to Father's Heart Ministries. There was the mother, who came from holidays and hurricanes. There was the older daughter, who never stole angels from a creche. And there was the younger daughter, who tied knots in loose lines (of fabric, wire, cable) as a reminder never to say the thing she wanted to say. Mother and father were, of course, getting on in age. Both at 65, their sheddings, coughings, and throat-clearings were general reminders to all within the vicinity of their rapidly decomposing bodies. For the younger daughter, aged 25, their senior moments were a constant source of anxiety and irritation. For the older daughter, aged 30, it was cause for nothing more than a sigh of the ugly, honest, entropic variety.

Whatever does it matter? Anyway.

Positively reviewed on every corner of the FluenSphere, critics praised *Daggers In* as "*the* quintessential whodunnit for a post-digital age." Featuring all of the hot content creators, the plot followed the lost codicil of a dead (by suicide: sorry for the spoiler, you should've seent it by now) dowager poet. *To whom shall the great bardess bequeath her estate?!* The 4 of them sat through the quasi-comical 12 cycles and 32 maunders-long yarn with bated breath and hardly ('cept the youngest daughter) saw it coming. They all agreed they'd enjoyed the movie, but each of them would remember it differently. And they'd remember it differently because of the long ride in the dark back to their timeshare.

Before we go any further, allow me to disabuse you of the expectation that something bad or interesting happens on this ride home. Not yet, and/or, not at all. Nevertheless, something in each of them changes. Maybe it's a kind of witness.

"Babe," said father to mother, "am I turning here? Where-mygoing?"

"Yeah hun," she said vexed by her smart-map, "merge up here. I think."

"Merge where? There's no merging lane."

"There should be one coming ahead. We wanna get on it."

"You know I can't see in the dark. I hate driving in the dark."

This was absolutely true. For some reason, the generally fearless old man hated driving in the dark. It's the one thing that made him *kind of* nervous. The one thing that made his nervous younger daughter feel, like, closer or biologically related to her father. I should also mention: It's possible the old man's fear of driving in the dark was the result of a recent cataract surgery and legal blindness in his left eye. But that's just speculation.

"Come on, city slicker," said mother in a warm and teasing tone. "You can't get us home?"

"I'll get us home, but I need you to guide us."

"I am!" she said, voice bouncing back defensively.

"Hey dad?" chimed daughter from the backseat.

"Yeah babe, whassup?"

"I can drive . . . you know . . . if you want?"

Indeed both children (four eyes between them, relatively healthy) were licensed to drive, but rarely bothered—accustomed to father and mother steering and navigating respectively. Also accustomed to the comforts of the backseat, its cupholders and climate control—and to the luxury and privilege of a kind of (backseat) driving that came with *knowing* how to do the thing they were witness to, but never actually doing it.

"Uh no," said father, unwilling to relinquish control to his untested 30-year-old baby girl. "I'm fine thanks." He'd been driving for almost fifty years. He wasn't going to stop now. He'd get them home safely. If mother would only tell him where to turn . . .

"Merge right. Stay in the right lane," said mother.

"I thought you said left?"

"Did I say left?"

"Mom has no idea what she's doing," said youngest daughter, suddenly ashamed of her outburst, but righteously indignant and ready to tell her truth. "Let me navigate. You don't even know how to work the phone!"

"Shut up, girl. I know what I'm doing."

"You have the phone upside down!"

"I'm reading it right! Trust me! *'Tate tranquila.* Merge left up here. The turn is coming."

"You reading right or left?"

"Left! *Puñeta!*"

"Uh oh, Mom said *puñeta*. You done it now," said older daughter. "You got her mad."

"Actually I think Dad got her mad."

"No it was you. When you said *'Mom has no idea what she's doing.'*"

"Why don't you just—"

"Make a u-turn up ahead babe."

"A u-turn?! It's a double yellow line. Am I not merging?"

"No hun, sorry, I was looking at the wrong part of the map."

"Hey Dad?" chimed older daughter again. "I said I'll drive. I can see just fine in the dark. If you want to pull over . . ."

"I said no!"

"Ok," she yawned. "Sorry I asked."

Younger daughter was visibly annoyed with her older sibling's show of false something-or-other. "You don't actually want to drive . . ." she mumbled in her general direction, but older daughter was already halfway asleep, the remains of a grin melting from the corner of her lips. "I know you're pretending," she said. "Pretending to sleep."

"Wheremygoing now, babe?"

"Make a u-turn when you can. We have to go south."

"You sure?"

"Yep. This time for sure."

"Alright," said father. "Alrightie."

////\ • /\\\\

Hard to say what each of them felt like that evening, but the four of them managed to get back safely (*praise Jesus*) and eventually pack for a quiet morning ride home through a charming flurry of powdery snow (previously forecast to have been a blizzard). They prayed before departing and the old man managed, with God's mercy, to drive them back to the city. The old lady, with God's guidance, managed to point them all in the right direction. The older daughter, with God's blessing, curated the trip's tunes. And the younger, with God's allowance, sat quietly and attentively behind her father.

Later that night, when the old man had finally slipped into his pajamas and found the ticket stub in his wallet, he remembered the way his older daughter (ever the dry wit) made him laugh when she mimicked the bardess in the throes of an accidental suicide. And the next morning, when the old lady cleared out her purse and found the ticket stub, she remembered how the child in the row before them thanked her sweetly for having helped him into his cumbersome bubble jacket. And a week later, throwing out a bunch of receipts and random tissues that had collected in her jacket pocket, the older sister found the ticket stub and remembered the way her little sis passed her a pack of hand-warmers in the middle of the movie (because her hands were always blue with cold). And a month later, when the younger sister finally got around to washing her clothes and found the wrinkled stub in the pocket of her jeans, she sighed and remembered having smuggled a plastic water bottle into the theater. *Selfish*, she thought, before uncapping a plastic bottle of organic green tea and gulping it down.

Black Spice Cake

The cake is dark as the perpetual midnight of polar winters where a reclusive poet will never visit, her soul veiled in the handmade lace of her own design, in other words, solitude. It's not seasonal affective disorder, rather, what modern folks call agoraphobia. Her companion, today, is a loaf made of nineteen eggs, five pounds of raisins, two pounds of butter, a pound and a half of currants, all baked in a milk pail. For flavoring, use five teaspoons of cloves, mace, and cinnamon. Don't forget to soak it in half a pint each of brandy and molasses.

Nowadays, we eat ginger chocolate ganache, rich and dark as a pile of velvet, moist as spring mud on your bare hands. Black spice cake takes too long, never mind banging the nutmeg by hand in the kitchen, then grating the scarlet seed-covering for mace. We bake persimmon fruit cake for the holidays, and pineapple upside-down cake in the summer. To serve a gathering, we make blueberry kuchen in a large baking pan or a strawberry trifle with lady fingers. The only significant marker of this mystical spice cake is its invisible attachment to a poet by a transparent, silvery cord.

The loaf, dense as the body of a planet sprinkled with carbon, ages in a windowless cellar for a month. Yes, I surmise the attitudes towards mold and mildew were more generous back then, more accepting of germs when the poet was alive. The black spice cake bakes five to six hours at a low temperature. In a poet's dream, every ounce of ground nutmeg changes into a blackbird in flight across the night sky. The spices traveled by ship from the southern seas, then cargo train from the panhandle, or maybe by ship all the way to the northeastern seaport.

Is the cake done yet?

The poet laughs.

What's so funny?

One, two more weeks, she says.

Slice by slice, I shall eat it with my fingers with a frosty glass of milk, right out of the ice box. The neighbors will press their noses against the window while I consume every nocturnal crumb, gazing into the kitchen with envy. I'll gorge myself on this cake while standing at the counter. I won't invite anybody in. I'm not anybody, after all. Who are you to gaze at me while I indulge in the pleasure of black spice cake, nineteen eggs and enough pounds of butter to sate the appetite for the rest of one's flesh-bound life. Bite on bite, I savor the thick scent of solitude, relishing this sweet treacle of seclusion.

At night, I dream of crystallized violets set atop fondant icing the color of licorice, tier after tier of fondant-dressed cake like a lacquered cabinet of sugar and spice. The poet appears in this dream wearing her famous white dress while carrying a platter of cake. Why do you pose such questions? she says, petulantly flinging up her hands. Have you visited the druggist? Has he given you a tincture of bromide for insomnia? Why else do the dark-eyed violets and poppies of the fields populate your sleep? In your dream, is black spice cake spelled as black spider cake? Do the spices morph into arachnids, those spiders crawling in the cellar of your unconscious?

All I want is my cake and eat it, too.
Nonsense.
Who are you?
Nobody.

Horseshoe

So I dreamt two horseshoe crabs were mating in the shallows and everyone gathered at the docks to watch and I could tell the crabs were so afraid and so in love and so in a hurry to get it all done before one of us could stick a hand inside and ruin everything. Not that they could hear us all there and the dinghies paddling in a rush to see. I don't think they have ears to hear but I bet they could feel us, ripples through the water, like. That stayed with me for days and days and we had nowhere to go, really, our house on a rock surrounded on all sides by water and diving birds and buoys. So one night I snuck into the compost bathroom with my phone and scrolled and scrolled and found the photos she sent me four years ago when I went a week away on business. She must've known how lonely I'd been even a day without her. The subject line read semicolon closed bracket ;] wink and I had no idea when I opened the message that my saint wife who'd grown from an ugly duckling into thank you Lord Jesus my gentle swan of a lover could arouse such desire. I trembled back legs jelly to my hotel every night for the rest of the week ready with those photos of her waiting for me to come home. Four years later and they were still gorgeous to me. So there I was in the compost bathroom and there she was again on my phone that glint of confidence in her eyes that smirk verging on sassy. I felt a wave of passion rise with a force enough to kill a whale, never mind the amorous horseshoe crabs in the shallows. I wobbled back to bed where she sat staring out at the moon on the water and the buoy with its bell in the dark. Beautiful, I said, showing her the pictures and laughing, it's you. It's just you. Beautiful. That's not me she said, hands over her chest over the violet furrow where her breasts used to be. You could make love to me tonight she said. But I didn't. And we hadn't since. She was right. And we slept back to back that night, two saints.

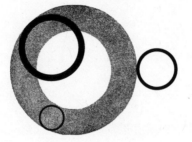

Deep Violet

The color of a bruise or a lotus leaf in shadow under the water.

The page of a notebook one has dyed by hand, watercolor.

The nameless face of a deceased ancestor who appears obscured
in a dream.

A scrap of silk one intended to use for a scarf, now rumpled
in a drawer.

The skin of grapes clustered on the vine in late autumn.

The shimmering cloud on the horizon off the sea cliffs.

The enhanced versions of infrared signals emitted by nebulae.

A wavelength shorter than blue and longer than ultraviolet.

The amethyst hue of vitilette sweet potatoes matching a cut geode.

The jagged furrow on a woman's chest, the cancer resected.

Not quite mulberry yet almost eggplant, lilac, or plum.

A gentian dye used to classify bacteria as positive or negative.

The silhouettes of dolphins swimming in pod by the shoals.

To evoke violet without using the word violet.

Arousing fond remembrances, as the lady writes.

To find a piece of deep violet or grape-coloured material that has been pressed between the pages of a notebook.

Olives and Roses

When I was fairly advanced in years, beyond the tumult of youth when a woman would experiment with drastic changes to her physical appearance, on the verge of menopause, I got a tattoo. I'd never permanently marked my body prior to this, never mind my skin. In my twenties, before any of the olives I'd pickled were famous all over the world—the black gold olives which made a fortune for me—I watched a vendor at a street fair and handed her a twenty dollar bill to paint a long-stemmed, thornless henna rose on my shoulder. The rose lasted for two weeks before it faded. I'd trace it with my finger every morning, wondering whether it'd last by night. When it finally vanished, I'd taken so many baths with scented almond oil that I'd almost forgotten it was there. I outlined the ghost of its presence with my finger, then looked in the mirror at the space on my skin where it had lived.

This tattoo, which I acquired as an older woman, was a remembrance of this other slender rose which floated less than a month's worth of days on my skin. The woman who painted it with her fine brush didn't say much as she worked quickly, dipping the brush tip in her mouth, then the auburn henna in a way that reminded me of the radium girls, who worked in the watch factories. Later, we learned that the girls—women, of course—were poisoned by the brushes tipped by radium paint. I was studying the history of maps then, not as a cartographer, but rather, as a budding poet. I had no idea that olives were awaiting my development of a new pickling technique in the near future, thanks to a job I'd take at the boulangerie, a cooperative bakery that specialized in fresh wolverines and shepherd's breads and loaves of rustic bread riddled with olives. Ate so much bread during those years, and now wonder whether these saddle-bags on my hips are the better or worse for it.

I imagine these saddle-bags filled with olives plucked from the trees of the world: the mission, the green, the black, the cerignola and kalamata like flesh, and the gold. I didn't bleed much when the tattoo artist inked my shoulder, although I'd been warned that I might. Though my skin has loosened like the cloth-bounded covers of a first edition volume of a medical glossary, he didn't complain much in inking the figure of the rose as I described it to him, which he first penciled in his sketchbook so I could see it. I nodded, yes. At least, that's how I remember it. I explained to him, it's neither nostalgia nor an attempt to recover a younger self. A young man with the air of an old soul from the sea, he merely nodded. Over time, the bodies he's tattooed are maps of roses entangled with lilies of the valley, smoldering volcanoes with their calderas of ash, rolling plains and pine forests. The map of my skin, an olive tree with a multitude of invisible, astringent fruit in its torso.

I will keep this rose tattoo, a map to the afterlife, unto my death.

Maelstrom

Today, even this hour, God's face is floating in the water where the lepers dip in and out of their skins marked by lesions and snowy disease, or is it a huddle of paralytics lying on the steps of a pool called Beautiful close to the Sheep Gate, the one near the colonnades? When Jesus walked the earth under olive and fig trees, an angel would stir the waters in this pool. You see, at the beginning of time, God had a face and still has one, although not many of us see it nowadays.

Age has nothing to do with this, as the God of ancients exists outside time.

In a maelstrom of wind and water in the darkness of genesis, before the arrival of shivering crowds at train stations or the surveillance of public baths by angels of vigilance, nothing hovered over the face of the waters until the face of God did so, a dynamo of monsoon wind and rain moving over the deep as a whirlpool until it morphed into a portal to an eye or the rose window of God.

Is an eyelid of God also a rose petal?

I suppose the water has a face, as well as God, who designed its waves—

Not the echo of drones in the future of war, but rather, the omniscient eye of God guiding a stream of souls, not guardian angels, enters a door the color of blood, cousin to the flowering ranunculus—a sacred bamboo called nandina in the southern provinces, with bright foliage and berries in the winter, the same color of heavenly bamboo at dusk—homeward. A red fox tail, sidling through the underbrush mingled with mulch, explores the vinegary scent of humans lingering in the night.

Meanwhile, the rose window draws hearts, says the poet in translation.

More precisely, it attracts the mind and inspires the emotions, or vice versa. Do you see any hearts in the darkness, adrift like red pontoons? Can you see their atoms of desire? Any sentient lifeforms, self-cognizant or not? The trial of a lonely heart is that you think it's going to be all about cats and paws from now until the end, in other words, the soft authoritarian reign of domesticated beasts like our feline friends—from cosy armchairs and litter boxes—will be our ultimate ruin.

Complacency survives in the remains of a displaced civilization and its disenchantments.

Rather, you're dissatisfied with everything under the sun. The lines of light spin you into a roaring maelstrom, right into the radiant bosom of God with a rose window of mullions in a giant cosmic rose etched with fine tracery reminiscent of an oculus on clear nights, where the hairpin streaks of the Milky Way adorn the sky. Let's not say it's like tinsel. You speculate whether or not this maelstrom could fit on the head of a pin or even a poppy seed you'd swallow in the blindness of an eye, and the whole universe would be inside you.

As we wait for a maelstrom, some angels stir the pool.

Iodine

In a time of war, a streak of horizontal lightning splits the sky from east to west, and a girl doesn't know whether it's a missile or weather. Her bones start to dissolve, and she doesn't know whether it's from radiation poisoning or nervousness. Lighting glows in an electric ball or a cloudy dome, trails her route to school. It glows atop ship masts in thunderstorms, rolls across abandoned train tracks like tumbleweed. In space, an astronaut has a blood clot in a jugular vein. The clot lodges in the astronaut's deepest vein like a ball of red yarn tightly wound around its spool, awaiting the analgesic touch of aspirin.

It's treated with blood thinners and pills. On earth, a fire-fueled landmass the size of ours is burning to a crisp—no mere seasonal bushfire—and the skies turn orange. This spectacle, like the skies of Mars, can be seen from space. What is the world as we know it coming to, or what have we made of it thus far? The raging flames, tongues of equal destruction for all, lick every combustible surface from termite-riddled wood to fresh eucalyptus skin.

A pyrocumulonimbus cloud, the noxious pillar of smoke the color of bromine and tangerines, is photographed from space, a plume fanned like a goose feather. A cumulonimbus flamma-genitus, it generates its own weather system. If this were an atomic bomb, first the flash and then the fallout would be witnessed miles away. Toxic ash carried through underground aquifers and rain-water tanks infiltrates the drinking water systems into the thyroid glands of women, poisoning the red-lobed butterflies glistening in their throats.

It takes months to diminish the activity of a hyperactive thy-roid. The little gland shrinks until nothing's left. All the seas of the world might hold more than enough mineral iodine to displace the radioactive isotopes, but it's too late for women's thyroids. In a matter of years, all the iodine under the sun is radioactive, and larks in the fields stop singing. Our bodies glow like radio-luminescent clock dials painted with radium. The gulls no longer drink salt infused with old-fashioned iodine when they fly over the waves.

Vertical flight, said the poet.

Our bodies, *earthly ruts.*

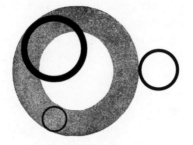

Needles

Indeed, these are dark times. There's sickness everywhere. I kissed you, not knowing it would be goodbye. And now in my lungs I carry what infection claimed you. I feel it. A cough no tea can cure. I knew the risk, but I couldn't have said goodbye without at least pressing my lips to the top of your kerchiefed head in that most ancient and queer gesture of intimacy. I suppose a gesture bourne of the reddish-brown sensitivity that trespasses the thin and supple membrane of our lips to find whatever infra-orbital nerve makes information of what we've touched—or has touched us. If I could or if we could map the nervous history of our lips to music, I imagine a kind of free jazz, the notes of which remind us of moments in our lives too powerful to have forgotten, but forgotten anyway. Unfortunately, and I should have known, despite choosing to take the risk and kiss you, I find myself resentful. Your propensity to falling ill. Your nail biting, which I told you was gross and dangerous and neurotic. Compulsively putting your goddamn hands in your mouth every so often like a child. And then to watch as you withered. Hacking up phlegm at all hours. A terrible catarrhal noise. All of it, undignified.

There's something about our desire to be witness to dignity. Dignified objects. That is, things and people outside of our own abjection that bear in their comportment a kind of put-together-ness. In my country, the constitution makes clear a distinction in governance between the *dignified* and the *efficient*. For centuries we've maintained the sacral role of a royal family as a means of preserving in our people a sense of dignity. Perhaps because our forebears knew the importance of model behavior. It's the prime minister and parliament that are entrusted by the people to be the *efficient*, curanderxs of socio-political uncertainty tasked with the mess of indignity that is our fallen condition.

The Lacrimal Order has its divine hierarchy. The Tribes and Clans; their chieftains and councils and patriarchs and matriarchs. In your country, of course, you have no royal family or hierarchy. Instead, you have what? Pop culture? You have actors and movies and actors who aren't actually politicians, but thespians, and movies that aren't news, but cinema. These, I think, have always been your royals, your *dignified*. And for all the time I've been in this country, my love of this place growing in proportion to my love for you, I think they've become my royal family as well. For all that they've shown me. All that they've shown us. Your insistence on that horrible Arthurian film from the 80s. The literary legacy of the King's singular sword and the old mage lamenting to the young enchantress that the one God comes to drive out the many gods. And the noir films, their dapper Dicks and femmes fatales.

My favorite, you know, were the heroes. And my favorite among the heroes was John Stewart, an architect chosen by the Guardians of the Universe to serve among their protective Corps and maintain order and stability throughout the cosmos. A kind of space cop. Deemed worthy by the immortal Guardians, John was given a Power Ring and entered into the Corps by reciting their sacred creed. *In brightest day / in blackest night / no evil shall escape my sight!* Something like that. What I always found interesting about John and others in the Corps lore was that their Power Rings allowed them, through sheer will and inventiveness, to construct whatever they could themselves imagine. The Ring allowed them to fly through space, swim underwater, topple skyscrapers. But the Ring was useless unless allowed time to re-charge in the light of its sacred source, the Lantern—kept on the distant planet of Oa where it was protected by the Guardians. John was only as efficient as he was imaginative and as pow-erful as he was proximal to the source of his strength. I always found that kind of poignant.

But holy moly did you love the movies. All of them. It was movies that got you going, that reminded you of something grand beyond yourself. Those gaudy old Biblical epics I think were your favorite. Wondering now and again, as though it were the most original idea you'd never had, if the G-d of Abraham had in fact presented Moses with a ravishing vision of a techno-pastoral-fu-ture in the burning bush (not consumed by its flame).

"How different could it have been from our own Christmas tree?" you wondered, marveling at the tree you'd decorated. "Aflame with a string of cool, flickering lights. Maybe God showed Moses our Christmas tree."

Indeed, the only thing you loved more than the movies was Christmas. And every year, before we dumped the tree, you collected from its driest branches a sachet of its most fragrant needles. This year would've made forty-three bags. But this year marks my first time stripping the branches, filling the pine bag on my own. You would've wanted me to, right? Keep the tradition alive? For as long as I have left.

You were always my *efficient*, anyway. Always good with decisions. Always running the cost-benefit analysis in a snap to share your measured verdict on whatever uncertainty. And now, what once seemed so obvious to you makes sense to me. If a tree falls in unpeopled woods, does it make a sound? "Of course," you said. "Of course it does. Who are we to deny the sentience of trees in the deep dark woods that live beyond us?"

Nerve

The word spindrift is fizzy in this epoch, not the spoondrift of sea spray but injected gas, the carbon dioxide of atmospheric greenhouses in a thermal manner of speaking.

A rafflesia, the fabulous corpse flower the same height as a little girl, was recently found by botanists in a rainforest. It reeks of gutters, of non-surgical debridement in the necropolis.

No one cares about ambergris except the poets of yore. A fixative for fragrance extracted from the guts of whales, it washes ashore in bone-colored stones.

Only one of the forefathers of a school or movement could get away with saying, *the sea is beautiful*, while more dazzling phrases —*the clear architecture of nerves*—surfaces in a later stanza.

In this age, we live nervously out of yellow boxes and red pods, two of the three primary colors. Our brains are pod-infused molds of flowering dark matter, while our algorithms and data-banks of artificial intelligence end up in black boxes.

Dendrites spark like forked lightning in these pods until a wetness draws perpendicular blue lines in the foreground, the intersecting polygons of experience we paint in squares and quadrilaterals.

Horses of pure nerve arise out of the foam, the forerunners of a sea patriarch who loaned his name to the hereditary condition where skin and bones adopt the symmetry of boxes.

If only we could step out of our cubes, walk around with the furred nonchalance of foxes and lynx, not in boxes wherein the dead flowers lie, so classically—

grape hyacinth, bellflowers, wilting irises, paper hydrangea, cornflower and asters, columbine and larkspur, sage, anemone (not the type that grows in the reefs), lobelias, myrtle, lupine, gentians, indigo, blossoming onion, love-in-a-mist, and starry eryngos.

Meteorite Oxide

It's Easter Sunday, say the bells, and spring itself attests to April. The dogwoods have returned, their pale flowers tipped red, and the mourning doves, their plaintive triads, but in my Quaker heart I feel this is the autumn of my ninth life. I suppose that's hard for anyone to understand. Not the old man to whom yesterday I promised a poem. He was from the south and supposedly knew, but did not care for, Borges's late wife. He and I, we sat by the water a while talking and kept the mallards company and I couldn't tell if he was just warm and lonely or flirting and hoping. In retrospect I think maybe he too had come to this cosmic waygate with hopes another would see him through. But no. He couldn't have understood. The unbearable fullness of this life, which has come to the end of the line, and the gratitude that succeeds it. I'm not sure many people would understand, really, that it's not the kind of life you share. Even, or especially, you.

At this community church I've started attending, they've found various ways for me to be active. One such way, this morning, will be a special recitation before the congregation, before the choir and a brief play, before the Pastor's sermon, before adjourning to a great potluck feast in the basement. This is, of course, the most important spiritual day of the year. The day we celebrate our Lord and Savior's triumph over death, his enduring demonstration of a quantum entanglement yet to be humanly replicated.

Just yesterday the choir leader, a stern but loving woman named Sophia, asked me to attend choir rehearsal that I might practice my recitation in concert with the singers. I kept her notes (along with my recitation) tucked somewhere in the book of Matthew. *For where your treasure is, there your heart will also be . . .* A passage I'd highlighted after having also found it in a fortune cookie. One of those *eureka!* moments of spiritual clarity—a moment of magical synchronicity that brought me humbled, not humiliated, before Christ and his word. Mistaking, as the old man had, some fantasy of love as companionship that maybe I realize now was never for me. Which is to say, I *misread* what I thought to have been a sign from God. A sign that our love was meant to be. An impression too strong to ignore. A dream one wakes from sad because it isn't strictly *real*. Whatever. That's why I'd highlighted it, in case you were curious. Don't care if I know or ever knew a thing about His will. Or mine.

Anyway, I tucked my notes for this morning's reading in my Bible and only this morning, picking it up again, did I notice a little slip of chartreuse green paper under a small stack of dusty books at the back corner of my desk. It was too bright, too oddly shaped to have just been a post-it, though I'd probably made that mistake a million times before. No, this was something else. A piece of paper deliberately cut to deliver a message.

It was a note you sent with a small chunk of meteorite oxide commemorating our last road trip through the desert. You insisted we stop at that blasted crater. You wanted the spectacle and I wanted to leave.

Trying. It's not often discussed as a Judeo-Christian ethos. Trying is a part of the enterprise. In every sense of the word. *Taste, and see that the LORD is good; blessed is the one who*

53

takes refuge in him. Trying as in testing what is new or other for divine equanimity. *Trying it out.* Trying as in attempting to overcome a challenge. *Trying your best.* My great sin was not trying. When things became trying. I stopped trying. But at least I know why.

I think often of Jonah, begrudging servant of the Lord. And I think of his condition, bitter til his dying day, as the burden of exilic living. But he's not just an exile, right? The way Moses, before he was a hero, had already been chosen as herald. There's a vectored appointment that can't be ignored. Jonah, after accepting the Lord's call on his life, had also accepted his role as missionary. He nevertheless suffered, as most exiles suffer, living in a bloody little town that never, even after divine revelation, stopped seeming to him wicked. I heard a pastor once say that the deliverance Jonah had hoped for, after having done his duty, never came because it had already come. His deliverance was, itself, the bloody little town of Nineveh, full of lies and crime. But I think it's unfair to say, ignoring the true discomfort of living in exile. The loneliness.

So you bought just one ticket to see the crater because I protested so vigorously spending money to witness this spectacle of awe and despair. It reminded me of the way we, with or without acknowledging its horror, admire the spectacular power of an atomic crater. Given enough time we can forget the absolute terror of obliteration and marvel instead at the aftermath, shadows burned into siding, concrete ruins and the rusted remains of yesterday's tomorrow gone horribly wrong. But it wasn't all that. You went. You saw it. We left. And shortly thereafter, I left. And years later you sent me this small fragment of the meteorite with the attached note in your neat, all caps, architect's hand:

HI PAL,

I HOPE IT IS A NICE DAY
WHERE YOU ARE AND
THAT YOU ARE FEELING
JOYFUL. IT IS SUNSET
AS I WRITE AND I AM

*THINKING OF OUR ROAD
TRIP. HERE IS THE PIN
AND ROCK FROM THE
METEOR I GOT YOU BUT
FORGOT TO GIVE. I'M
GLAD YOU WERE THERE
EVEN IF YOU PROTESTED
THE PRICE. I THOUGHT
OF YOU WHILE LOOKING
AT THE CRATER.*

Reading the letter now I find myself full of longing, on the verge of tears, because I took for granted what your love meant to me. I took for granted that you had been my deliverance all along. On the backside of the note you wrote:

*P.S. THANK YOU FOR
EVERYTHING, AS YOU
KNOW.*

Never let die the part of you that feels abandoning love an unforgivable sin. But never deny a call on your soul. A calling is a calling. It cannot be escaped. And my sense now, as it was then, all disappointment and heartbreak aside, is that I heard the call and went when and where I was required. This is the faith journey I've undertaken. And faith is nothing if not the humbled acceptance of life's opacity. Because we trust in the Lord. Which is to say, no, I don't understand how or why we grew so far apart. But I've made peace with it.

Still sometimes I wish you were here to share moments like these. Moments I think you'd appreciate. Once upon a time, you'd have been the first and last thing I saw on Easter Sunday. But this morning, the air wet and cool, the sky gray and forbidding, the first thing I saw, just outside, trotting down the middle of the road, was a silvery creature too large to be a dog, too small to be a wolf. Its wildness, as it were, gave me pause. It both frightened and intrigued me. And when I froze in place, Bible in hand, it too stopped and turned its feral gaze on me. I saw myself small in its obsidian eyes. And then it grinned, a wide, toothy grin, before trotting onward over the crest of the hill.

Sea Organ

While I take this stroll on the sea cliffs at dawn, a scallop is apparently filled with sleepy dregs of moonlight, as it lives off a rugged shoreline.

This is one anonymous shellfish in a line of a thousand scallops my mother loved to eat since girlhood to her present decade, the soft muscle of molluskan flesh sandwiched between calcium carbonate plates, a set of tea dishes made in the ocean.

It's tea for two.

Take the moonlight and put a piece of it in my mouth, a communion wafer directly out of the hand of the universe, on my tongue. It dissolves with the thinness of flour and water.

It's a bivalve of moonlight like mine, swimming through the benthos of the deep amid mussels and clams by fanning its shells like wings.

Male and female, the chosen ones who are born hermaphrodites send their eggs and seed into the water at once, their microscopic spawn mingling with seagrass, each one mouthing invisible pearls of nothing to the moon.

If you're looking for a metaphor to graft onto the ridges of this shell, it could lie quietly in the arms of the moonlight, whispering fugues and figures of speech in the fragments of a grand narrative, a metaphysical whole no single eye can see in sum.

The moonlight hums a wordless music, the sea organ of its underwater pipes blowing like a wind ensemble warming up with scale exercises before a concert, little bellows of sound.

It's often said, the moon has a weathered face, whether it belongs to the rabbit under the cassia tree, the woman who drank the elixir of life, or a fat fish who drifted behind the hills.

I say, the moon is an embouchure without a face.

It's the mouth of a musician floating in ether.

From this aperture issues the color of pearl, the nacreous music of the spheres, a fragmentary narrative about our genesis in the mineral kitchens of creation, of God's flame singing on the elemental burners of the universe.

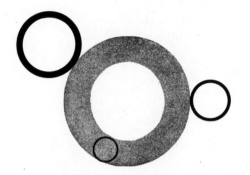

Serigraph

Here, the wind has a body, picks up glass and whips between the I-beams cutting fat from the land. What remains is slowly worn away by the unerring parsimony of what the tribe describes as ophidian for its serpentine shape, reddish color, and potency. But the wind is what *they* call it. So the wind is its proper name.

The thing about knowing, they started to say. And began again, whispering, *If we knew, should we have spent our days dry and crying that it would end this way, or high on trying to keep the good thing a secret?*

They never smile. They never cry. In hours where the wind whipped glass, inspired hiding in most, they approached and every time as breath hushed back onto the papillae of your tongue. Now, every time the wind whips through, it calls you backward to an elsewhere you sit wrongly inside of.

I. *I* sit wrongly inside of.

////\ • /\\\\

"Would the defendant please identify the object on display?"

"A print. Serigraph print."

"And would the defendant further identify the print? Artist, date, provenance, if possible?"

"It's an original. Thiebaud."

"Thiebaud?"

"James Thiebaud. Artist. The piece's titled *Black Spice Cake*. Dated 1970. Number twenty-three in an edition of fifty. A gift from a friend."

The print stood on an easel, angled so that both bench and committee might see it clearly. In the cool light of the courtroom its age was apparent, yellowed considerably over the years with creased corners and frayed edges evidence of its handling. Less apparent, trace remains of the deceased on its surface, earlier identified by forensic specialists. The black and white silkscreen trembled as if naked on the stand. *Black Spice Cake*, the object of scrutiny for a host of onlookers, judicial and otherwise, ready to draw over the drawing of their decision.

$$////\backslash \cdot /\backslash\backslash\backslash$$

The windows, short and narrow like loopholes, stretch alternately up from the floor and down from the ceiling. Just visible are the northern Graymere peaks, tall and dark and jutting high into the atmosphere. These aren't in fact mountains, in a geological sense, but the high wall of a crater rim. The work site is situated on breccia at the center of a tremendous, mineral-rich impact crater. Our place is hidden, we think, in the hills ascending the south rim. They are standing by a window, surveying the landscape the color of cinnamon, milk, and butter.

"You try and make a home here or anywhere, but it's just another rest stop before moving on." I manage to say this without crying. "You said that. Remember?" And they tried, sincerely, to make this a home for us. On the walls, festooning the windows, is a trellis teeming with non-native flora, vines crawling up to the ceiling and flowers blossoming out of season in every shape and color like birthday cakes.

They sit beside me on the bed. They have no need for clothes, for suits, for masks. They are the color of cocoa powder, bittersweet warmth, covered with sugar glitter. And laconic. They speak almost exclusively through haptic connection so that their words and thoughts happen inside. Their haptic empathy on the small of my back to say, *I can't believe we're cake. We are all made of cake.*

"Last night I dreamt that the panic formed a mob and found us," I confess, tearing up. "I can't live like this."

The longer we linger in dreams, the more difficult they are to translate into full speech. The thing about knowing, they started to say. And began again, this time a touch softer, *If we knew, should we have spent our days crying that it would end this way, or high on trying to keep the black spice cake a secret?*

I press myself into their cocoa-colored belly, round as a cupcake, and they reach around feeling for the smooth place where I, too, might have been human instead of angel food, and I shudder with hunger, afraid.

I press my lips into their neck, feel their warmth, feel them hum syrup through me, resonating everywhere inside until we lift, and we're floating above, my lips tacky with their brandy-flavored skin which fills me, goes down smooth like chocolate yet fiery like allspice. Breathe. I open my mouth and breathe. Swallow. To where they're warmest and softest. I bare my teeth, bite tenderly, and the vibration intensifies, desire surging between us on the outskirts until they pour mouthfuls of sweet cream on my lips, on my chin, and I want to drown in it.

/ / / / \ • / \ \ \ \

"A friend," said the prosecutor, pretending to turn the word over in his head. "You must have known," he continued, pulling what looked like a pen from his pocket. "Your friend was different. They are different. Different from you. Different from me." He twirled the pen between his fingers. "It's bad enough that you were in violation of zoning restrictions. But you took it a step further, didn't you?"

"Objection, your honor. Improper conduct."

"Sustained."

"My apologies," said the prosecutor, grinning. "I return to the evidence, to what the defendant has identified as '*Black Spice Cake*, an original serigraph print by artist James Thiebaud. Dated 1970, one of a set of fifty. A gift from a friend.' Is that correct?"

"Yes."

"And was the print prominently displayed?"

[ ]

"Objection, your honor. Leading."

"Sustained. Keep it up and you'll be held in contempt of court."

"My apologies, your honor. Where was the print hung?"

"Over the bed."

"Would the bailiff please dim the lights?"

Once the room was sufficiently dimmed, the prosecutor clicked his pen, kindling a black light. He trained his light on the print, revealing white spatter invisible to the unaided eye. The prosecutor clicked off his pen and signaled for the lights.

"What we see here are trace remains of the deceased. Their 'blood', high in disaccharides sucrose and lactose, is surprisingly sweet to taste, bio-chemically speaking," he said to the committee. Turning back to the defendant, he continued, "You must have known, as we all know, that they are a different tribe, made of different stuff. Layered, in fact, like a Napoleon. Part pastry, part cake, lots of layers. We all know what a Napoleon is, right? Mille-feuille, some call it. I'd wager that none here are averse to pleasure, and certainly not desserts. Generally speaking, however we find it, pleasure is a part of life," he said, glancing deliberately at the artist's print. "So what happened? Are you cake, too?"

"Objection, your honor. Hearsay."

"Overruled. Answer the question."

"I ate them."

"Why?"

"Because I love them."

"Was consent given by the gullible?"

"I—I don't—"

"Was consent given?"

[ ]

"Answer the question."

"Yes—"

"But they don't identify as singular and they don't distinguish between first and second person. They can't express consent in legal terms 'I, the undersigned, hereby consent . . .' So what makes you think this was something they wanted? What makes you think this was a voluntary offering of their collective body?"

"They don't—they loved me and I loved them."

"And at what point did you realize they'd been consumed by your 'love'?"

[ ]

"Since when is eating cake an act of love?"

[ ]

[ ]

"You must have known what you were doing?"

[ ]

[ ]

[ ]

Incunabula II

Jim had to admit playing the infield was kind of fun. Middle infield, or sometimes third base, offered him the opportunity to be quick, agile, even spectacularly acrobatic on occasion. Like that one time, out of sheer frustration, he barehanded a chopper down the third base line and fired it to first for the last out of the game. Or that other time he worked a hidden ball trick into a double play. Flashes of brilliance no one could deny.

Hitting, on the other hand, he found less amusing. Tee ball was a bore. There was no challenge to any of it. Fortunately the coach had reassured him that they'd start soft tossing during batting practice and he was eager to see what he could do with a little bit of spin and velocity. But if there was one thing he really loved about baseball, it was the moment after practice or a game where his dad would take him to get soft serve ice cream or a dirty water dog. Maybe even a sports drink if Dad was feeling generous. And it was always on this walk back to the house from the parade grounds that they were able to speak frankly as men.

"Dad," he started, "everything feels off."

"How so?"

"Things are changing for me. It's not the same. Not fun. Ya know?"

But how could he have known? He was an adult. He could do whatever he wanted whenever he wanted without pressure from parents or teachers or babysitters or grandmas. Jim could see his father pondering the thought while his cleats click-clacked across the sidewalk and the ice cream began to run down the side of the cone.

"Are you worried about first grade?" his dad finally asked.

"A little. What's it like?"

"It's fun! You'll learn cool new things. You'll meet cool new people. You'll love it."

"But . . . what if it's not like with Ms. Evans in kindergarten? I really loved it there. I miss her. And Larissa. And Michael. It was like the best time of my life."

"But you cried every morning when I dropped you off."

"Because I get bad separation anxiety. You know that!"

"So you're saying the best years of your life are behind you? You peaked at three and now, some two years later, you look back on those halcyon days with wistfulness?"

"It's all downhill from here, isn't it, Dad. This is the beginning of the end."

Apples and Satellites

We are made of apples and satellites in a garden edged by flashing swords, and those apples change into parcels of information when we bite into their skin. As surveillance robots in outer space, we radio bits and bytes to earth. In the darkness of apples, our data bounces around in the electromagnetic field, and our panels shine with the glory of ancient scrolls read aloud by prophets of yore.

The stardust of our universe glows in apples like the jewels of satellites.

Our organs are composed of apple guts, and the russeting of summer orchards. We are rust-colored, chock full of seeds to the very core, just like apples. We're often green and small, some-times red, even yellow or golden as those in the markets say: pink ladies, gala, honey crisp, or galaxy. In the microcosmos of a widget engine, we use applets to run small applications to guide apples on their data-bound journeys through the skies.

Apples sing of expanded knowledge, those brassy orbs of information:

We are satellites orbiting the world—
     in the vast mystery of the alpha and omega,
apples take after pinpoints in the cosmos,
        smaller than applets running in widgets,
lesser known than a sunrise
     witnessed by astronauts. We radio good news
of rainstorms and the motion
        of eschatological weather
where the rarest apple tree in the world
     adds rings to a record of two thousand years,
bearing pink-streaked fruit of tart flesh
        like the rose of the world to come.
We grieve what we know in this life—
        and celebrate what is to come.

A Happy Medium

I first saw her the Sunday after my quinceañera set up a table in the neighborhood at dusk. A small woman perched on a corner bathed in gold and dying light. Mami warned me she was no good. Or not that she was no good but that she had been misled and had chosen to mislead others. But Mami's warning wasn't enough to keep me away forever and two years later the summer before I went off to college I visited the small woman's table.

"Finally!" she proclaimed. "Welcome, Ms. Mayra."

To my great astonishment the small woman Mami warned me about already knew my name.

"How did you . . . ?"

"That's a lovely necklace," she replied, grinning and pointing. "Was it a gift?"

I'd forgotten about the necklace, my name in gold cursive dangling from a thin chain.

"My mother," I managed.

"You don't have to be nervous," she said, smiling graciously. "Have a seat."

So I sat and she dealt cards I'd never seen and I was nervous the whole way through like I had to pee. Nervous because my mother could find me at any moment. Nervous because I didn't know what to expect from this small woman. Nervous because finally at seventeen-eighteen I'd chosen curiosity over security.

The cards were spread across the table in a perfect grid and featured fascinating vignettes and icons. There were some swords. Some stars like the kinds kids used to draw on their binders. There were some knights. Some horses. A regal old man seated on a throne. And the devil. The only card we all recognized. Demonic emblem of the entire enterprise. What kept my mother awake weeknights and full moons. Here was laid before me the one thing she spent her best years trying to protect me from. How quickly and easily he'd come to cross my path.

Perhaps noticing the Ghost as it swept through my sinner's heart, the small woman lifted a hand and said, "Not to worry. The important card here is the Emperor, seated on the throne, smack dab in the middle. I'll explain the devil in a moment. But first the Emperor . . ."

She went on to tell me about a fated encounter with an authority figure. Charming and well versed in the ways of the world, this person or thing would occupy a central place in my life. The devil, she continued, was there to remind the querent (me) that an obsession with the material details of one's circumstances could never lead to happiness. I couldn't imagine my mother would disagree. I thanked the small woman and when she didn't ask for compensation I offered what I had in my pocket.

"Seven bucks ok?"

"That's fine, Mayra. You are kind, thank you. I wish you all the best this year with college."

"Thanks," I said reflexively, unsure whether I'd told her about my plans or she'd read that too in my necklace.

////\ • /\\\\

I visited her again when everything went south with the be-loved professor and my own life had taken a bit of a nose dive. She was right. He was everything I thought I wanted in a man. Charming. Worldly. Bold. Always wore a blazer. A consummate lover. But not for me. He was aggressively intellectual. Preten-tious. Insecure. Domineering. Competitive. All of the graduate student teaching assistants it seemed were in competition for the singular affection of their beloved professor, the last known aco-lyte of the great deconstructionist.

Marc. His name was Marc. Whenever Marc would deign to invite me out with his coterie of frenemies, he treated me like a know-nothing. Having a laugh at my expense for not know-ing the obscure works of Heinrich Von Kleist or Anne Desclos became a sport for him. So I ended it. I had sense enough to end it anyway. I'm not stupid. Truth be told, I got a real kick out of cracking his porcelain ego. Then trampling it in front of his colleagues.

After I explained all of this to the small woman, she shrugged, smiled, and asked "How's your mother?"

"My mother?"

"Yes. How is she?"

"She's fine, I guess. Why?"

"Just asking," she said. "How about a reading?"

I nodded, trying not to appear too eager for the devil's fore-knowledge.

This time she drew a regal woman on a throne. A heart pierced by three swords. A man and woman holding hands under an angel. And at center, a woman suspended between heaven and earth, surrounded by a wreath, one of the four cor-ners each of the card featuring the head of a man, an eagle, a lion, and a calf or bull or ox. This card was upside down.

////\ • /\\\\

The next year, when all of the seniors were scrambling, I decided to apply to the nation's top rated Divinity School, and, to Mami's great joy, I was accepted. This would mean my moving.

Ready for a new beginning and spurred on by my favorite Paul Simon track, I made a new plan, dropped off my keys, slipped out the back, and hopped on a bus for a radically liberated future. But I hadn't anticipated the loneliness of my newfound freedom.

This I explained to the small woman over the phone.

"Don't you miss your mother?" she asked.

"Yes, I suppose," I said. "Why do you always ask about my mother?"

"Just curious," she said. "That's all."

"Will you read for me?"

"Of course, sweetheart."

I couldn't see the cards as she drew them. All I could hear was a shuffle of laminated cardstock, her soft, indiscernible humming, the sound of a little girl calling for mommy. And after some time, perhaps spent reading, perhaps spent tending to the small sound behind her, the small woman said, "The flag on this one's shoulder, on this one's back, is only pretext to a condition. This one has no nation. And here, the people see in them no future, only a present from which is extracted affect and labor. Still, this one is waiting for life. For love. Waiting for someone to share a star with. For someone who might see, anyway, what lives beneath the mirror surface. This one is lion-hearted. This one. Is holding a cup just for you."

So this one I waited for.

Insect Algorithm

The new populace adores the ringing sensation of a sleek autonomous sensory meridian response, the tingling on your scalp when an electrostatic wind runs its phantom fingers through your hair in the high desert, ironically, at a resort with the name palm and springs tagged. The greenhouse gases over the past few centuries have raised the temperature by a degree or two. No more oasis for the inland empire, only deserts: free-flowing water in the empirical wilderness is a mayfly ghost.

Or it's the frisson down your spine while you shiver as the names of unrequited loves are whispered under the snow moon late in winter, although still early in the year. Those lost loves are chitinous husks to the wind, elusive as aphids silvered by lily water. As it blows down the feverish hillsides in the language of the foehn wind, an algorithm of the dead brightens the hours of those who wish to live in the past, logged into anti-angst generators driven by artificial intelligence.

To pacify a nervous populace, each week, an insect algorithm in the desert metropolis coughs up a new game of crickets for the disquiet and unsettled, a new puzzle for the perpetually restless and wingless to ponder. Today, the formula is simple. It's a comparator or a superlative phrase, plus a noun, then a descriptor mixed with language exhumed from the crypts of obscurantist poesia, as in the following lines:

truer than	saffron	dipped in absinthe
sleek as	aphids	silvered in lily water
wetter than	a cloud	soaked in roach milk
wetter than	aphids	dipped in absinthe
truer than	a cloud	silvered in lily water
sleek as	saffron	soaked in roach millk

Where does the insect algorithm find data for its puzzles? Scavenging the verbal microportraits of the population, the anti-angst generator compiles tiny mosaics for these language games. Simultaneously, it also serves as a surveillance tool of subpopulations whose collective portraits were compiled into a data cloud. Who are you in the midst of things, and where? What are you doing, and why? The words form pictograms of neural pathways sparking and fusing all at once like a female katydid's brain picking up forewing vibrations in a tree.

As the story goes, the big data operates like a mega-constellation of insects that amateurs on this planet can't see with their telescopes. The starlight hitting our eyes is ancient, taking billions of light years to travel since the beginning of the universe, far older than the keys that turned inside the locks of ships constructed of wood from eons ago, or anything we could describe in our quotidian experience. When sculpted by massive data visualization scripts, this aggregate face of verbal microportraits was apparently no less than the visage of a giant beetle.

Watch II

This is what happens. When promise learns loneliness and mediocrity understands its necessity and the tables have turned on the prodigious and the adopted lay awake in adulthood not quite contemplating but bleeding inside from their smallness in a world gathering itself at the seams of a natural and unseemly order. You don't have to squint and cock your head to see the sense in its brutality. But what was it Marco Polo said to the melancholy Khan at the end of the world? . . . *cercare e saper riconoscere chi e cosa, in mezzo all'inferno, non è inferno, e farlo durare, e dargli spazio.* Which seems a considerate measure in a hyperloop packed elbow to elbow, shoulder to shoulder, surrounded by the vast darkness of the tube beyond. I could use some space. Some topside air. A break from the adolescent explaining to his friends that he expects his relationships to remain *transactional.* At first he sounds a bit too wise for his age. Almost convincing . . . *in the beginning she does all the things you like. Then, after a while, she stops doing the things you like, but still expects you to do all the things she likes.* Then, trying to be both cheeky and impressive, comes his turn toward the brutal. *I need her to understand this is transactional, baby. I'm transactional.* His friends are indeed impressed by the word. *Transactional.* They laugh reverentially at his insight and repeat the word. *Transactional.* I want to turn and remind him that love and capital exchange are not quite the same. But I realize it's not my place. He seems like the kind of kid who'd enjoy a good conversation, who's waiting for someone to match wits, but it's not my place. Sadder still, I don't have it in me to say what should be said. Because, yes, what he says makes absolute sense. He understands the brutal order of *things.*

Careful not to aggravate the other sardines, I twist my wrist just clear of my coat cuff to check my watch. And I almost can't believe the blue dot approaching at uncommon speed from behind. I turn, as gently as I can, to see what I can see. But in the densely packed loopcar I can only make out a gradual shifting among the sullen heads of other passengers enthralled by the same conversation. Someone moving like a shark beneath the surface, parting water, a bullet along the break, cutting across a wave.

Then there you are, emerged from the sea of sulking sardines to arrive at a point apart from me, no longer red or blue, but here and flesh. And you're so focused on those boys, so ready to set them straight, that you don't yet see me. So I take a moment to secretly study your face. The shape of your shoulders in tight space. The light on your pursed lips like a dream. Until I can't help myself.

Hello, I say.

Here we are.

And you finally see me, standing behind those boys, and you smile a brightness an order of magnitude greater than the sun. Almost more than I can bear. Almost.

Hi, you say. Hi.

Having forgotten whatever it was you meant to tell those brash boys about true love.

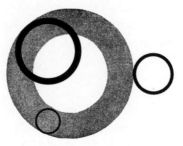

The Golden Plaque

On the other side of the universe, there is an archivist whose age is older than the total number of annular rings in most ancient sequoia on this planet. She has lived through the seasons when the world as we know it in history suffered through plagues and long, grotesque wars. In one sleeve, she keeps an inkstone. In the other, a goat's hair brush. Her archive is arranged in an order that no one except the alpha and omega knows. Once upon a time, her goat's hair brush started growing mysteriously, a slow lengthening like the soft, angelic hair on a girl's head—lighter than the fur of a goat, and she prayed that it would stop because then she could no longer keep it in her sleeve if it grew too long. It stopped, and she tied it with a ribbon.

Her jumbled archive of miscellaneous objects is lost to this world, and no one will ever find it—this brings her no solace. Her consolation is writing from the inventory of odds and ends, the flotsam and jetsam on this side of the universe, the object histories with their bizarre rhizomes and forked lightning, their labyrinths of topiary shadows tossed into the exosphere beyond the orbit of weather satellites, those little sisters to space exploration carrying golden plaques with an image of a man and woman, the man with his hand raised in a greeting, and pi, the golden ratio, and a diagram of their home planet in relation to the sun.

Out these mystical archives float the moth-eaten myths and mossy dreams which God used to seed our imaginations and edify the warning dreams of our prophets, the souls of image-bearers who may, in fact, never encounter forms of life other than their own. These twin golden plaques, exact copies of one another, on satellites headed to the spaces between star fires, tell the stories of humanity, if other intelligence exists to decipher them several million years from this moment. Once upon a time, there was a world, and in this world, there was love. This is why God made us. There is snow falling this very hour, dusting the stone ruins in Athens where ancients sought beauty and wisdom in poetry and riddles, now even in Jerusalem as men and women push their books and daily bread in carts. The archivist waits patiently for God to tell her it is time now to put down the brush, go to sleep. It was all a nocturnal dream of image-bearers creating more little images in a house of mirrors *ad infinitum*, forgetting their human origins in the divine source of love. There is much data with the expansion of knowledge yet also much forgetting during the millennium. *Do not forget,* she whispers, holding her brush. *Do not be afraid. There is much to remember.*

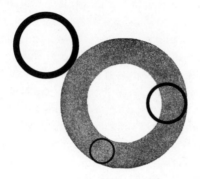

Property Plot

Souvenirs is a catalogue of strange objects that commemorate fictional places—and each of these souvenirs tells an oblique story about the narrator. Each of these souvenirs is indebted to previous works of literature, visual art, film, music, architecture, design, history, and/or performance. Find below the various sources of inspiration for each of these stories.

Watch I: "Skunk Hour" by Robert Lowell

Photographer's Cloth: "The Man-Moth" by Elizabeth Bishop

String: *Le Mont Analogue* by René Daumal

Flock: "A Cure of Souls" by Denise Levertov

Gazeless: "The Man Who Sold the World" by David Bowie //

from ""Stanzas, Sexes, Seductions" by Anne Carson: *My personal poetry is a failure. / I do not want to be a person. / I want to be unbearable.*

Foil: "God's Grandeur" by Gerard Manley Hopkins

Space Rock: *Watchmen* by Alan Moore, David Gibbons, John Higgins

Black Jade: "The Fish" by Marianne Moore

Stubs: "Knives Out" dir. Rian Johnson

Black Spice Cake: Recipe by Emily Dickinson

Horseshoe: "Clingstone"; Narragansett Bay; Jamestown, RI

Deep Violet: from"Things that Arouse a Fond Memory of the Past"in *The Pillow Book of Sei Shonagon*: "To find a piece of deep violet or grape-coloured material that has been pressed between the pages of a notebook."

Olives and Roses: "Map" by Wisława Szymborska

Maelstrom: "The Rose-Window" by Rainer Maria Rilke

Iodine: "The Lark" by Gabriela Mistral

Needles: "The English Constitution" by Walter Bagehot // "Green Lantern/John Stewart" created by Dennis O'Neill & Neal Adams

Nerve: "Early Mondrian" by Frank O'Hara

Meteorite Oxide: The Book of Jonah //various Coyote narratives

Sea Organ: "Breakage" by Mary Oliver

Serigraph: "Half Cakes" by Wayne Thiebaud

Apples and Satellites: "What Women Are Made Of" by Bianca Lynne Spriggs

A Happy Medium: Rider-Waite Tarot (Major & Minor Arcana)

Insect Algorithm: "Securitization" by Ange Mlinko

Watch II: *Invisible Cities* by Italo Calvino

The Golden Plaque: "Pioneer Plaque" by NASA on Pioneer 10 and 11

The headers of *Souvenirs* are set in Sabon, an old-style serif typeface designed by the German-born typographer and designer Jan Tschichold in the period 1964–1967.

The body is set in Futura PT. This sans serif was designed by Paul Renner in 1927. It was created as a contribution to the New Frankfurt Project and based on the simple geometries that became representative of the Bauhaus style. Renner was not part of Bauhaus but he shared their beliefs regarding fonts as expressions of Modernity.

Andrew E. Colarusso is author of *The Sovereign* (Dalkey Archive Press 2017) and *Creance; or, Comest Thou Cosmic Nazarite* (Northwestern University Press 2019). He was editor in chief of *The Broome Street Review* from 2009 to 2017.

Karen An-hwei Lee is the author of *Phyla of Joy* (Tupelo 2012), *Ardor* (Tupelo 2008) and *In Medias Res* (Sarabande 2004), winner of the Norma Farber First Book Award. She authored two novels, *Sonata in K* (Ellipsis 2017) and *The Maze of Transparencies* (Ellipsis 2019). Lee's translations of Li Qingzhao's writing, *Doubled Radiance: Poetry & Prose of Li Qingzhao*, is the first volume in English to collect Li's work in both genres (Singing Bone 2018). Her book of literary criticism, *Anglophone Literatures in the Asian Diaspora: Literary Transnationalism and Translingual Migrations* (Cambria 2013), was selected for the Cambria Sinophone World Series. She currently lives in greater Chicago.

Fiction

A collection of visions shared across time and space, *Souvenirs* is a collaboratio
between authors Andrew Colarusso and Karen An-hwei Lee that celebrates frag
ments from the literary afterlife. A philosophically astute, poetically searing col
lection of miniature fictions and contemporary fables, *Souvenirs'* objects take o
shapes of their own designs creating a composite map to a world populated wit
little transparent souls and ghost ships in lost bottles; a menagerie of curios; pho
tophores of bioluminescence humming in the depths: light begetting light, dee
calling to deep. In these twenty-seven prose gems, it seems that Colarusso an
Lee are writing from a single mind as they strike a balance between humor an
philosophy; the acute and the everlasting. The ideas they discuss—religion, faith
universality, continuance—are large, but their prose is accessible, and at time
as hilarious as it is profound. Strange, compelling, and arcane considerations c
watches, jade, seaweed, and cake, among many other items, come through wit
stylistic prowess and earnest, intelligent consideration. *Souvenirs* adds complex
ity to the mundane, re-centers the iconic, and gifts the reader with nothing sho
of astonishment; wonder baked into each delicious slice.

"More than almost any book I could name, *Souvenirs* possesses the virtue c
re-readability. Its stories move so delightfully and surprisingly, and with such curi
ous effects, that they provoke not only a first look but an immediate second."
— Kevin Brockmeier, *The Ghost Variations: 100 Storie*

"*Souvenirs* is a field guide to nowhere, to beyond the deep dark, the end of th
beginning, that is, to the untethered imagination. Read it and be unboxed!"
— John Madera, *Nervosities* and *Among the Dynamo*

"A mystical archive, at once whimsical and grave, these dark charms conjure
by two contemporary Scheherazades, attempting to forestall world's end, and i
communion with the saints: Borges, Calvino, and so many others, linger in the min
Recalled in a variety of registers, these traces—souvenirs of the dissolving world—
so hard to hold—haunt and fill us with longing." — Carole Maso, *Mother & Chil*

"These [stories] move like luminescent, bewildered sea creatures through the 'toxi
ash' of cyber sea time. They hover like rainwater and clutter our hearts like goos
feather. It's a collection born from two amphoral voices. Their union designed t
be a vertical flight' into the unknown and a 'rafflesia, the fabulous corpse flowe
the same height as a little girl.'"
— Vi Khi Nao, *The Vegas Dilemm*

A RED OCHRE EDITION

121 California Ave
Reno, NV 89509
BAOBAB PRESS   www.baobabpress.com

$14.95
ISBN 978-1-936097-41-8
51495>

9 781936 097418

BONNIE HAGEMANN • LISA PENT
AND THE MEMBERS OF WOMENEXECS ON BOARDS

THE COURAGE TO ADVANCE

Real Life Resilience
from the World's
Most Successful
Women in Business

"Read this book
and be inspired."
PAUL POLMAN,
Co-founder of IMAGINE